PRAISE FO

Tom Clancy fans open to a strong female lead will clamor for more.

— *Drone*, Publishers Weekly

Superb!

— *Drone*, Booklist starred review

The best military thriller I've read in a very long time. Love the female characters.

— *Drone*, Sheldon McArthur, founder of The Mystery Bookstore, LA

A fabulous soaring thriller.

— *Take Over at Midnight*, Midwest Book Review

Meticulously researched, hard-hitting, and suspenseful.

— *Pure Heat*, Publishers Weekly, starred review

Expert technical details abound, as do realistic military missions with superb imagery that will have readers feeling as if they are right there in the midst and on the edges of their seats.

— *Light Up the Night,* RT Reviews, 4 1/2 stars

Buchman has catapulted his way to the top tier of my favorite authors.

— Fresh Fiction

Nonstop action that will keep readers on the edge of their seats.

— *Take Over at Midnight,* Library Journal

M L. Buchman's ability to keep the reader right in the middle of the action is amazing.

— Long and Short Reviews

The only thing you'll ask yourself is, "When does the next one come out?"

— *Wait Until Midnight,* RT Reviews, 4 stars

The first...of (a) stellar, long-running (military) romantic suspense series.

I knew the books would be good, but I didn't realize how good.

Buchman mixes adrenalin-spiking battles and brusque military jargon with a sensitive approach.

13 times "Top Pick of the Month"

HONOR FLIGHT

AN NTSB / MILITARY TECHNOTHRILLER
STORY (PREVIOUSLY PUBLISHED AS
"GALAXY")

M. L. BUCHMAN

Buchman Bookworks

Other works by M. L. Buchman: *(* - also in audio)*

Thrillers

Dead Chef
Swap Out!
One Chef!
Two Chef!

Miranda Chase
Drone*
Thunderbolt*
Condor*

Romantic Suspense

Delta Force
Target Engaged*
Heart Strike*
Wild Justice*
Midnight Trust*

Firehawks
MAIN FLIGHT
Pure Heat
Full Blaze
Hot Point*
Flash of Fire*
Wild Fire

SMOKEJUMPERS
Wildfire at Dawn*
Wildfire at Larch Creek*
Wildfire on the Skagit*

The Night Stalkers
MAIN FLIGHT
The Night Is Mine
I Own the Dawn
Wait Until Dark
Take Over at Midnight
Light Up the Night
Bring On the Dusk
By Break of Day

AND THE NAVY
Christmas at Steel Beach
Christmas at Peleliu Cove
WHITE HOUSE HOLIDAY
Daniel's Christmas*
Frank's Independence Day*
Peter's Christmas*
Zachary's Christmas*
Roy's Independence Day*
Damien's Christmas*
5E
Target of the Heart
Target Lock on Love
Target of Mine
Target of One's Own

Shadow Force: Psi
At the Slightest Sound*
At the Quietest Word*

White House Protection Force
Off the Leash*
On Your Mark*
In the Weeds*

Contemporary Romance

Eagle Cove
Return to Eagle Cove
Recipe for Eagle Cove
Longing for Eagle Cove
Keepsake for Eagle Cove

Henderson's Ranch
Nathan's Big Sky*
Big Sky, Loyal Heart*
Big Sky Dog Whisperer*

Love Abroad
Heart of the Cotswolds: England
Path of Love: Cinque Terre, Italy

Other works by M. L. Buchman:

Contemporary Romance (cont)

Where Dreams
Where Dreams are Born
Where Dreams Reside
Where Dreams Are of Christmas
Where Dreams Unfold
Where Dreams Are Written

Science Fiction / Fantasy

Deities Anonymous
Cookbook from Hell: Reheated
Saviors 101

Single Titles
The Nara Reaction
Monk's Maze
the Me and Elsie Chronicles

Non-Fiction

Strategies for Success
Managing Your Inner Artist/Writer
Estate Planning for Authors*
Character Voice
Narrate and Record Your Own
Audiobook*

Short Story Series by M. L. Buchman:

Romantic Suspense

Delta Force
Delta Force

Firehawks
The Firehawks Lookouts
The Firehawks Hotshots
The Firebirds

The Night Stalkers
The Night Stalkers
The Night Stalkers 5E
The Night Stalkers CSAR
The Night Stalkers Wedding Stories

US Coast Guard
US Coast Guard

White House Protection Force
White House Protection Force

Contemporary Romance

Eagle Cove
Eagle Cove

Henderson's Ranch
Henderson's Ranch*

Where Dreams
Where Dreams

Thrillers

Dead Chef
Dead Chef

Science Fiction / Fantasy

Deities Anonymous
Deities Anonymous

Other
The Future Night Stalkers
Single Titles

ABOUT THIS BOOK

(Previously published as *Galaxy* in the USA Today bestselling anthology *Origins of Honor.*)

A C-5 Galaxy, the premier heavy transport jet in the US military, and its secret cargo lie shattered across one of America's largest military bases: Joint Base Lewis-McChord.

Some say it crashed. Others say domestic terrorism... Or a declaration of war? They need answers and they need them fast.

Miranda Chase, air-crash genius, and high-functioning autistic, and the National Transportation Safety Board's newest investigator, gets the call. But unraveling the real cause could cost her honor or her life.

1

APRIL 2004

"Mooney Three-five-three-Charlie-Victor, Boeing Tower."

Miranda was less than a hundred feet in the air after taking off from Boeing Field in South Seattle when the tower called her.

That was unusual.

The final time she typically talked to the tower was when they gave her clearance to proceed onto the active runway and take off. After that, they just wanted you out of their traffic pattern and gone. But that was definitely her airplane's N-Number.

"Three-Charlie-Victor. Go ahead, Tower." Though it always bothered her that N-numbers was shortened after the first communication. She'd never met another Three-Charlie-Victor, but she could. And then what might happen? But air traffic control was always about efficiency.

She was on a straight-out departure to the north because the wind had shifted in the six hours since her arrival *from* the north. The morning breeze had died, and the spring warmth of the early afternoon now beckoned.

Straight out would lead her above Harbor Island and out over Elliott Bay with an amazing view of Seattle to her right. Seventy miles to home on Spieden Island in the San Juans. In her Mooney M201—the fastest production propeller-driven plane when her father had bought it twenty years before—she'd be home in twenty minutes.

"Remain in pattern right. Depart south over the reservoir tower. You are redirected to JBLM."

"JBLM? Did I hear that correctly, Tower?" Even as she responded, she turned right and raised the landing gear once she came parallel to Boeing's runway heading south.

Change was unnerving. She supposed that's why they called it change.

One moment she was in the midst of her planned routine, her visual flight rules path from Boeing Field to Spieden made a clear, easy-to-visualize map for the next twenty minutes of her life. Then there would be putting the plane away; and it wasn't too late for planting her cabbage and broccoli starts.

But her planned routine was now changed without any warning.

"Roger that. Joint Base Lewis-McChord," the tower repeated clearly.

"But I don't have clearance to land there." JBLM was a massive military base. Nor did she have the charts. She checked in her nav computer, but all it showed on her screen was "Restricted Airspace" and the most basic information about the field.

Flaps from takeoff to cruise.

The Mooney was fast enough she'd be there in under fifteen minutes. Well under.

"Contact their tower on 119.325."

She punched the frequency into her second radio as they read it out. "Roger that."

"And, Miranda?"

"Yes, Tower?"

"Thanks for all your help with the crash."

"You're welcome," she supposed was the right response.

She never knew for certain.

Mom had taught her that when in doubt, "Thank you" and "You're welcome" were both reasonable responses. She'd been right. They generally worked well —as the second option had appeared to this time.

She came abreast of the abandoned water tower that hundreds of pilots each day used as their turning point and headed forty-five degrees left out of Boeing's flight pattern. She supposed it wasn't abandoned in actuality, as so many pilots depended on it even if the water department didn't.

She'd been called to Boeing Field for her first-ever solo accident investigation as an IIC—Investigator-in-Charge—for the National Transportation Safety Board. Technically, she was a specialist in commercial aviation rather than the small planes of general aviation. But dispatch had said, "Well, you're handy. You're the only one in the Seattle area today."

With the Mooney, she'd arrived from her island in under half an hour. Boeing field had still been closed to all traffic, but when they'd found out who she was, they'd given her special clearance to land. The runway was so long—a major testing and final configuration center for the Boeing passenger jets—that she'd been given clearance for a midfield landing.

She'd stayed high enough to not disturb the site of her pending investigation, which dangled near the start of the runway.

It was a curiously intact site, though she'd had to wait almost three more hours to access it.

A set of high-tension power lines hung well north of the runway. They were clearly marked with bright red balls clipped on at consistent intervals. Also, they were well below the proper flightpath.

Furthermore, Boeing Field had glideslope indicator lights that would have shone red-over-red indicating the pilot was too low.

Yet somehow, the little Cessna 152's pilot had managed to snag a wheel in the thick power lines. Rather than tearing down the line and probably killing himself, he was left to dangle over fifty feet in the air, upside-down for four hours. The power company had finally shut down the feed to much of the area—including the Boeing factory hangars. Then they had to wait for a crane big enough to retrieve the pilot and then the half-ton plane from where it hung tangled in the power lines.

Miranda supposed the plane remaining hooked to the wire was a testament to Cessna's robust landing gear designs.

By the time he was down, she had all of the interviews completed: tower, plane rental, and eyewitnesses (of which there had been seven). She'd secured a copy of the tower recordings as well as the air traffic control readouts.

Once it was down, she'd inspected the plane for faults —at length—which had greatly upset the pilot who she'd made wait.

People were the strangest element of all to her. Why didn't they ever understand that she was ruling out all other factors, aside from pilot error, *before* their discussion?

Apparently, this pilot didn't either.

He seemed very upset when she tried to question him.

That part hadn't gone well. But she'd been able to have the FAA reopen airfield operations quickly—after she'd taken a flight herself to prove that the glideslope indicators were working properly, and it was the pilot who had malfunctioned.

It had been his fault and her report would say so.

When she communicated that, he became even more upset and one of the airport security personnel had to restrain him.

It made no sense.

Her review had been impartial. But she now understood why investigators were told to never disclose a report's conclusions until it had been fully reviewed by the NTSB. She wouldn't forget again.

In fact, she made a mental note to fully reread the entire legal background of the NTSB this week—starting with Section 5 of Public Law 89-670 which established the Safety Board in 1967.

She'd always known that people would be the hardest

part of the crash for her, but it was too small an incident to require assembling a team. So, she needed to see what aspects of the law could help her in the future.

But that was for later. Instead she would focus on whatever reason she was being called to JBLM.

"JBLM Tower, this is Mooney Three-five-three-Charlie-Victor."

"This is Gray Tower. Go ahead."

"Three-Charlie-Victor inbound from Boeing. I was told to contact JBLM Tower on this frequency."

"There is no JBLM Tower anymore. State purpose."

"What do you mean there isn't…"

That's when she saw the column of smoke. It was right where the McChord Field should be—south-southwest at thirty miles.

It wasn't a small fire. Great billows of black smoke were blooming upward. Even as she watched, there was a fresh explosion and fireball on the ground. More black smoke gouted upward.

"We're busy here, Three-Charlie-Victor. Stay clear of this area. This is not a civilian channel."

But she'd been told to call them. Until she knew why, she couldn't really think of what to do next.

Maybe it was because her call hadn't been properly addressed.

"*Gray* Tower, this is Mooney Three-five-three-Charlie-Victor."

There was an audible snarl over the air. "What part of *leave* didn't you understand, Three-C-V?" Which was a wholly improper shortening of her callsign.

"This is NTSB I-I-C Miranda Chase, reporting as requested."

"NTSB? What the— Hang on." It was a good thing he'd stopped himself. The Federal Communications Commission frowned on obscenity per Title 47, Part 73. Perhaps military rules were different. More to add to her reading list.

Five seconds later he was back, and being very polite. "McChord Field is closed at this time... We'll vector you to Gray Army Airfield... Be careful in the pattern as we're handling a great deal of overload traffic... A helicopter will be waiting to take you to McChord." She could just hear the voice in the background stating instructions for the radio operator to transmit. It seemed an inefficient methodology, but she supposed that it worked for them.

"Roger. Three-Charlie-Victor awaiting direction."

And as he guided her into restricted airspace, Miranda couldn't take her eyes off the conflagration at McChord.

Her first-ever time as Investigator-in-Charge had been one of the very smallest production airplanes built, caught in a power line.

She spotted the massive T of the empennage that had broken free from the McChord crash—as so often happened with the tail section in major accidents.

Six stories high and nearly twice the width of her Mooney's wingspan, it was the T-tail of a C-5 Galaxy jet transport—the largest plane in the entire US military.

It appeared to be the only part that was intact.

2

THE HEAT WAS STRONG, EVEN THROUGH THE HELICOPTER'S windshield.

The fire still blazed hot despite the vast array of fire equipment gathered around it and spraying water and foam.

Miranda wished that they only used the latter. Water damaged so much of the evidence she would need to make a determination.

The helicopter pilot had wanted to fly her around the perimeter of the wreck, but that wasn't how she worked.

Terence, her mentor at the NTSB Training Center, had helped her formulate a methodology that allowed her to approach a crash in a layered fashion that didn't overwhelm her. Most investigators could deal with the chaos of multiple factors, but she never understood how they did that.

When it finally became clear that the pilot was going to fly around the whole wreck anyway, she'd shut her eyes and waited. She could feel the lateral forces acting on the helicopter and her body as he circled. Her eyes remained tightly closed until the forces neutralized and she could sense the slight weightlessness of a descent toward a final landing.

"You're a strange lady, Lady," the pilot said as he set the small OH-58 Kiowa helicopter down on its skids well clear of the fire.

"I know." Every kid she'd ever met growing up and every adult now that she was grown had echoed that sentiment.

Almost everyone.

Her parents never had. Nor her governess, who'd become her guardian after her parents' deaths in an air crash. Nor Terence her mentor. But the examination board members of the NTSB's newly formed Training Center certainly had, even as they'd passed her with the highest marks of their first graduating class.

Miranda climbed down and the helo departed.

Should she be surprised that she was suddenly alone in the middle of one of the nation's largest military bases without an escort? She wasn't a soldier. She also wasn't an airwoman. Were there any Navy here at JBLM? Because she also wasn't a sailor or a Marine. But she didn't think so. So it would be okay with them that she wasn't a sailor or a Marine without an escort in a secure area. That was some comfort.

She turned her back on the fire as she pulled on her custom-tailored NTSB vest—even the small-size standard-issue ones fell off her shoulders and hung halfway to her knees. No one designed for a woman only five-foot-four.

The six-inch fluorescent-yellow letters across her back would announce her purpose here.

Then she began checking each of her pockets carefully to make sure everything was in its place: notepads, recorders, measuring tapes, and all the other tools of her trade. It was. Then she hung her NTSB badge prominently around her neck.

She was ready.

With her back still to the fire, she pulled out a weather meter and checked the readings.

The fire was playing havoc with the winds. She hated to do it, but could only record "light and variable" with any certainty. She assumed that the tower would have more accurate records...except hadn't they said there *wasn't* a tower anymore?

She looked around but didn't see one.

There was something in the heart of the fire that might be the stump of one, but she couldn't be sure.

Nothing in the NTSB Training Center's curriculum had mentioned what to do if there *was* no control tower. Actually, they did, for an uncontrolled airfield. But for major airports there were supposed to be control towers from which to gather essential information.

The fire was hot enough that even at this distance the air thermometer recorded a seventeen-degree Fahrenheit difference in the open versus shielded by her body from direct exposure.

How was she supposed to make sense of this? Even

the simplest task was so difficult. It took her three tries to slip the sensor back in its pocket. And the notation in her notebook was barely legible—it was so bad that she blacked it out completely and rewrote it in careful block print.

Once she had completed that, she knew what she had to do.

It was time to implement Terrence's made-for-Miranda layered strategy.

Weather.

Not quantifiable beyond "Clear sky. Winds light and variable."

Terrain.

McChord Field was a big flat airfield designed for heavily laden warplanes to land. No mountain they might have run into or had to avoid at the last moment. "Terrain clear. Pavement dry."

Debris.

The next layer was to circle the site of the wreck and locate the outermost extent of the debris field. She had the little green perimeter marker flags in her backpack. She had her camera and drawing materials in her vest so that she could create a map of the outline.

But there was only one of her.

And there was between four hundred and sixty thousand pounds (empty) and nine hundred and twenty thousand pounds (maximum takeoff weight) of airplane spread over more than a mile of runway. And a tower.

Even as she watched, the firefighting Striker trucks were running over the debris and destroying even more evidence.

"Who the hell are you and what are you doing here?" someone shouted at her.

Miranda sighed.

She had no idea.

3

"MAJOR, SHOW SOME RESPECT," A GENERAL STOOD CLOSE beside the man who had addressed her.

"Yes, sir," Major Charleston—by his oak leaf insignia and the name stitched over his right breast pocket—didn't sound happy about it. He was tall, which made it easier not to meet at his eyes.

Instead she focused on the stitching of his name—heavy black embroidery stitched directly onto the pocket of his camouflage uniform. The left pocket had "U.S. Air Force" stitched just below a patch depicting a pair of wings.

He was a pilot.

"Your insignia are brown rather than gold. Is that so that they don't reflect light?"

He tried to look down at his collar points, but his neck didn't bend that way. "Yes. No. Hell if I know. Look, Lady—"

"Major," the general quelled him with that single

word. "I called in the order for an NTSB investigator to be requested and if you look at her badge, that's what she is."

"*I'm* the Air Force investigator. I don't need anyone's help."

"You certainly arrived fast enough, Major. I was told the closest USAF crash investigator was in Nellis. That's why I called the NTSB."

"I was passing through, returning from Alaska. Besides, she's twelve," the major protested.

Miranda knew she was young. And being five-four and having Mom's slender build added to how inaccurately people perceived her age without ever thinking to ask. Besides, she was *not* twelve. That was inaccurate by sixty-seven percent.

Terence had taught her what to say. She always thought it sounded like bragging, but he'd insisted that she learn it by rote.

"I have dual masters from the University of Washington in Materials and Aerospace Engineering. Top of my class. I graduated from the NTSB Training Center at the top of their first-ever class. And I've been studying airplane incidents since I was thirteen—including reading every NTSB Aviation Accident Report ever published."

Terence had told her to say the last line sarcastically, but she'd never figured out how to do that.

This time she didn't even say it. She would leave the major to draw his own conclusions about his degree of qualification versus hers.

General Elmont, he'd stepped from behind the major

and she could see his name tag now, chuckled softly, "You tell him."

"My name is Miranda Chase. I'm the Investigator-in-Charge for the NTSB." Another rote phrase that Terence had trained her to use at the start of an investigation.

"Son," the general clapped a hand onto the major's shoulder. But they didn't look anything alike, and they didn't even share a last name. "Thought the Air Force would have trained you better. First, this was a Dignified Transfer flight and you're not being very dignified."

Miranda wondered what disaster had needed a plane as huge as a C-5 Galaxy to transfer that many military coffins. She hadn't heard of any disasters in those escalating wars in Iraq and Afghanistan.

"Second," the general continued, "never, ever be rude to someone—especially not when she's smarter than you."

Or perhaps they were bringing back a few coffins but were mostly empty; returning to gather more troops and equipment here at JBLM to take overseas. That seemed more likely.

No!

No hypotheses.

She would make her observations, then gather other facts. Then, typically without the clutter of hypotheses, she'd arrive at her conclusion.

The major snarled out, "This way!" as he stalked off toward the wreck where the fire was now mostly under control. Actually, the two wings that had broken free were still towers of flame and smoke, but the fuselage was coming under control.

The general stopped her with a light hand on her arm.

Miranda looked down at his hand.

He was touching her.

Right there.

Touching her.

No one touched her.

Not lightly.

If felt...like she needed a shower—a hard, driving one with the spray turned up as hard as it would go.

The touch was there, but it wasn't.

Too light.

But she could feel it.

She knew that the problem was hers, not the touch's. But she couldn't block it. She didn't know what to do.

All she could think about was the touch.

Even on a warm summer night, she'd layer on extra blankets for the weight because she needed contact to be firm.

She'd—

General Elmont's hand slid away. "...so you might want to forgive his manners."

"Whose manners?"

The general leaned closer to inspect her and she kept her eyes on his two stars—silver, shiny. "Major Charleston."

"What manners was Major Charleston exhibiting that I'm supposed to forgive him for?" She struggled to reconnect the pieces.

The general blinked hard several times, as if he too had lost the thread of the conversation.

"Why don't you go follow the major? We'll talk later. Take care of my men. That, Ms. Chase, is an order." He turned and walked away. He was limping badly and there appeared to be blood caked on the back of his pantleg. Fresh blood now darkening even more of his pantleg.

But he must know that.

Miranda turned to follow the major.

4

MIRANDA MOVED TO WHERE MAJOR CHARLESTON STOOD close by the lead fire engines. The pair of massive Oshkosh 3000 Striker firefighting engines were easing toward the fuselage. A bumper-mounted nozzle was blasting a cloud of water and foam at the aircraft.

"Look, Lady," the major shouted over the roar of the vehicles' six hundred and fifty horsepower engines but kept his attention on the fire. "I'm head of the site investigation team for the military. You do not have the clearance to be here. Because the general ordered it, I'll put up with the risk of having you on site, but you stay right at my side or I'll—"

"I'm cleared to Top Secret."

The major spun to look at her. "Say that again."

She'd never understood the purpose of repeating herself.

When she didn't answer, he spoke again, proving that he had heard her the first time. "I have only Secret-level clearance. Since when do they give NTSB people *Top Sec—*"

"I've had it since I was eleven. My father said it was more convenient and the government agreed. I'm not quite sure why. I never thought to ask and now he's dead. I'm just entering my second five-year reassessment. Why is the general bleeding?"

"He was a passenger. He's the sole survivor of the C-5 Galaxy's crash, alone at the very rear of— Wait! Why is he *what?*"

Again the request to repeat herself. Instead she turned and the major turned with her.

General Elmont hadn't moved far from where they'd left him. The general was kneeling on the ground and fell over sideways even as they watched.

"Shit! You! Stay here!" He aimed a finger at the ground and then rushed toward the general.

Miranda shuffled over the one step to stand exactly where Major Charleston had pointed, then turned back to inspect the firefight.

Because of the tunnel vision created by the two massive fire engines to either side, all she could see was the fuselage. Now the debris field was no longer her focus, but rather the remains of the C-5 Galaxy in front of her.

The fuselage rested at an unusual angle. It wasn't rolled side-to-side, but its rear section was pressed hard against the pavement and the nose rose over two stories higher than it should. The front had ridden up over a structure that must have once been the control tower.

The massive wheel carriages dangled helplessly in midair.

The nose gear appeared to be planted in the remains of the control tower.

The heavy roar of the two Strikers actually created a comforting pressure. Though she did pull earplugs from their vest pocket and firing range earmuffs from her site pack.

The massive hull rose in a three-story tube. Even with the tail and wings broken off, two hundred feet of the plane remained mostly intact.

Miranda had never seen an aircraft incident while it was still in progress.

The flames around the outside of the hull had been suppressed, but fire still shot out the open end of the fuselage where the tail had been ripped off.

Easing forward, the two Strikers extended their long, folded, rooftop booms. At the end of either boom was a slender, carbide-tipped nozzle almost as long as she was tall. Even as she watched, they extended the nozzles and punched them through the hull, high on the curve and fifty feet apart.

Inside, she knew more evidence was being destroyed as they pumped six hundred gallons per minute of water-foam mix. Or perhaps it was a water–Purple-K suppressant mix.

The flames pouring out the few openings in the hull diminished rapidly. She'd moved forward with the Strikers to see as much as she could before they washed it away. The radiant heat still poured off the sides of the plane.

On one of the exterior compartments of the Striker to her right, she spotted the label PPE. Inside were reflective-foil Personal Protection Equipment suits. She pulled one on, including the foil cowl that covered her head and draped over her shoulders. Miranda selected a breathing bottle.

That was much more comfortable.

The Strikers had stopped the flow from their front-bumper sprayers and were focused on fighting the interior fire with their injector nozzles.

She crossed in front of one truck and began circling the wreck.

Miranda had learned to be polite to drivers when they stopped for her when crossing the street. She never knew if them stopping because of a red light entailed her to acknowledge those drivers as well. As they hadn't run her over by running said red light, she had determined that it was a low-effort trade-off to wave at them anyway.

Having learned her lesson, she waved to the Striker's driver and engineer as they stared down at her past the three high-speed windshield wipers to combat all of the back spray.

They waved back.

Perhaps a little more excitedly than she'd expected, but she was always a poor judge of such things.

5

INSIDE THE C-5, THE FLAMES WERE RETREATING.

The two piercing nozzles were still running, spreading great quantities of foam over everything until the few remaining flareups looked like bonfires in a snowy Purple-K suppressant-lined cavern rather than a raging conflagration.

Mounds in the foam were curiously uniform. She stopped to inspect one.

A foil-clothed fireman rushed up to her.

"Are you okay?" Their shouts were muffled by their PPE gear.

She shouted that she was. *Why wouldn't she be?* But she couldn't seem to hear her own voice inside the mask, so she nodded enough to move the foil cowl and the breather mask as well.

"Jesus. Don't scare us like that." He shoved a helmet on top of the foil. It slid down over her ears.

"This isn't a safe zone."

She knew that. Why did he think she'd borrowed the protective gear?

Two teams of firefighters had arrived on either side of them. They wielded hoses that suppressed the last of the flames around her and punched ungainly, lurid holes in the field of purple foam that had finally stopped raining down from above.

Once they moved away from her, Miranda inspected the holes.

Through one was a patch of red. Through another dark blue, with part of a star scorched dark brown.

Flags.

Flags *on coffins*. That's what the rectangles were. The general had said it was a Dignified Transfer flight and she was pleased to confirm that piece of eyewitness account with verifiable hard evidence.

More holes appeared through the melting foam.

Scorched flags on *many* coffins.

The coffin ends toward the rear of the plane were mostly unburnt. The fronts were scorched to a near uniform brown.

A few were burnt through, exposing the steel, transfer coffins that were chained down to the decking. The chains crisscrossed in an X-pattern on either side had anchored each coffin exactly in place despite the hard crash. Three columns across the width of the deck. And the number of rows hidden by the ongoing firefight.

Miranda proceeded forward, inspecting the variations on each coffin.

Occasionally the firefighters would shout something incomprehensible through their masks. Then a group would cluster around her to continue chasing the fire forward.

Sometimes they blocked her way forward, but they soon moved forward again. That freed her to continue her inspection of one coffin after another.

The scorching of the more forward coffins' flags was asymmetrical. She wanted to take pictures, but her camera was beneath her foil suit.

As was her flashlight. C-5 Galaxy aircraft had very few windows. There was the light from the gaping hole where the tail had been torn off. And ahead the way was lit only by the rapidly disappearing firelight.

Here, in the middle of the aircraft's long cargo bay— longer than the Wright Brothers first powered flight—it was now quite dark.

Inside the suit it was terribly hot and sweaty—mostly from her own trapped body heat, she knew—but the firefighters were all still wearing theirs. Perhaps it was better if she remained in hers.

She also couldn't get out her notebook to record the precise tie-down points for each set of chains. It took her a moment to work out an mnemonic so that she could recall the layout later.

Miranda had proceeded halfway up the long cargo deck and the destruction grew worse with each step.

Here, the coffins rarely had more than tatters left of their flags. Some of the cases were knocked askew by massive bending of the floor plates. The decking of a C-5 Galaxy was an integral structural element, not an additional surface as in several other military transports.

Flexion of the plates meant flexion of the hull. Some of the stresses were near critical failure.

The ceiling above had burned through.

The rear half of a C-5's ceiling contained a passenger seating area.

Typical configuration: seventy-three rear-facing airline seats. The interior ladder was still folded up against the ceiling.

Major Charleston had said that the general was the only survivor.

She would have to inspect the upstairs, but she knew that if there had been any passengers, they would have been cooked by the fire directly beneath them.

No survivors.

They could wait. As dead as the men in the coffins.

Miranda looked rearward to estimate how high she'd climbed so far. At least ten or fifteen feet above the rear loading—

6

"No!" Her shout echoed inside her foil hat and breathing mask.

She scrabbled at the edges and tore them off.

The air was hot and stank of burnt fuel, but it was breathable.

Once she was clear of the PPE's headgear, she did retain the helmet as the overhead structure no longer looked reliable.

The helmet slid down so far without the foil padding that she had to wear it practically on the back of her head in order to see.

She raced downslope toward the rear of the cargo deck.

"No!"

Miranda's feet glissaded on the thick foam.

"Stop!"

The six men silhouetted at the rearmost row of coffins ignored her...until she slid helplessly into them. Her transfer of momentum was sufficient that while she came to a stop and remained standing, three of the men went down.

As they fell, a brand-new American flag fluttered out of their hands and draped over the last puddles of Purple-K fire-suppressant foam remaining at the tail ramp.

Several of the men cursed, but one of the ones remaining upright grabbed her arm.

Solidly. As if to steady rather than restrain.

"Thank you, I'm fine now." He let go.

The team had removed two scorched flags and had already replaced one of them. Though now the three men were soaked, wet with the water still flowing down the decking and patches of foam on their fatigues. They looked unhappy as they regained their feet.

"What are you doing?"

They all looked at each other. "We are reflagging these coffins and then transferring them properly," the sergeant who'd steadied her assured her in what she supposed was meant to be a soothing voice. Peters by his pocket stitching. Master sergeant by his sleeve device.

"No, you aren't."

"Yes, ma'am. We are." Less soothing. "Do you know what's inside these? These are fallen men. Their families are waiting and we—"

"The burn pattern on these flags is evidence in the crash and they are not to be removed."

"By whose orders?" Sergeant Peters was sounding stern.

"By mine."

"And who are you?"

She'd only ever practiced her rote phrase for the beginning of an investigation. Of course, this was only the second investigation she'd ever done, so perhaps it would be okay to repeat her introductory narrative.

"My name is Miranda Chase. I'm the Investigator-in-Charge for the NTSB."

The sergeant looked at her wide-eyed for a moment, then shook his head before signaling for his men to continue.

They were ignoring her.

No!

She couldn't have that happen.

Again.

Like everything else in her life.

But she was *the* Investigator-in-Charge.

Even the general had agreed with her.

The general had—

"I've been ordered by General Elmont to take care of his men."

That stopped the flag detail as they were unchaining the first coffin from the deck. The flag was beautifully wrapped. It was big enough that it was far wider and longer than the coffin. The long sides had been folded underneath, then cleverly tucked into the overhang at the head and foot in such a way as to make a neat cap over the whole. She almost stepped forward to pluck one of the corners apart to see how it was done.

But everyone was looking at her.

Why?

Oh. "Yes. And per General Elmont's order, I was doing just that. Now stop what you're doing. I need to have the foam cleared away from the more forward coffins so that I can photograph them properly. And you might want to send a man up the ladder to see how many more are dead in the passenger compartment."

In unison, all six men turned to look at the ladder folded up against the ceiling, which was thirteen feet and six inches above the deck. It would have been sufficient if one or two had looked. Miranda certainly didn't waste any effort repeating her earlier action.

The sergeant waved two men to go see. Then he had someone run for some brooms and a hose. In moments, she was once again moving upslope, forward through the aircraft.

After she shed the rest of the PPE foil suit, she had a team of four men brushing clear each coffin and then getting out of the shot as she took photographs and made notes.

By the time they reached the middle of the aircraft— where she'd turned around earlier—the fires were out and the foil-covered firefighters were leaving.

One stopped close beside her and dragged off his breathing apparatus.

"Are you the crazy bitch who just walked into an active fire?" His fury was evident, even to her.

"My name is Miranda Chase. I'm the Investigator-in-Charge for the NTSB. I've been ordered by General Elmont to take care of his men." She tried combining the two explanations into a proclamation.

"Fucking lunatic, more like."

Unsure what else to do, she picked up the foil cowl

and breathing apparatus that she'd dropped on the deck and handed them to him.

He looked at them as if he didn't know what they were.

"I would like to keep the helmet for now. You are correct about the plane's structural integrity being questionable."

"Jesus," he shook his head. Whatever his perceived duty was, he had apparently discharged it by invoking a deity. Or perhaps the son of one. There was apparently some debate regarding the invoked's true status though she'd never taken time to research it herself.

7

THE COFFINS COVERED THE ENTIRE LENGTH OF THE PLANE'S long cargo bay—twenty-five rows of three coffins each.

"Going to need nine body bags, sergeant," one of his men had returned from the upstairs passenger area.

"Roger that."

"Make sure that they're photographed in place," Miranda told him.

"Have a heart, ma'am."

"They're already dead. I surmise that they won't care."

The man turned away quickly—perhaps to more rapidly achieve his task. Yet he didn't move to do so.

"We also know that there are still at least seven crewpersons unaccounted for," Miranda reminded him. "They will need body bags as well."

"Jesus," the airman whispered just as the fireman had —in a way that didn't seem appropriate for someone seeking spiritual guidance or supernatural assistance.

Finally Sergeant Peters muttered out, "Just do what she says, Airman."

"If you say so, Sarge."

As they continued forward, the fire damage to the coffins increased. Flags were almost completely gone. Char and smoke damage darkened the burnished metal.

Then dents. Front panels bowed inward, indicating an explosive overpressure. She took measurements for future calculations once she'd determined the bending force pressure necessary to displace a sealed metal coffin's structure.

Some coffins were knocked askew despite their heavy anchor chains.

At the midpoint of the aircraft, the circular frames that made up the cavernous arch of the hull were bent where the massive wings had broken free from the structural wing box.

But near the bow, other forces had been at work. The integral steel deck bent and warped. The hull's frames were not only out of round, but flexed differently from the ones near the wing support box. Perhaps due to the upward bending force of the nose section.

All of Miranda's training hadn't prepared her for this. In its fifty years of service, the C-5 Galaxy had only suffered seven Class-A hull-loss incidents and three of those had been due to ground fire.

A Class-A loss was defined as over two million dollars in damage or the death of any personnel. This plane cost over two *hundred* million and even though the majority of its passengers had been dead to begin with, more had died.

Definitely Class-A.

There hadn't been any major hull losses of any

commercial or military planes during her training, so she'd never seen one in person before. She had studied every single one in the past though.

And military.

She'd known that her security clearance—one of only three IICs to have top-secret clearance—would probably involve her in future military investigations. But this was her first.

The plane. She would focus on the aircraft.

Through a gash in the plane's skin, she could see tumbled and shattered concrete blocks. Presumably the remains of JBLM's control tower.

"The problem is…"

"What, ma'am?" The sergeant was close by her side.

The response surprised her. There hadn't been time to assemble an NTSB team. She had no structural specialist, systems specialist, human factors, engine manufacturer rep, Lockheed manufacturer rep, or any of the others to confer with.

They would all be here. Probably soon. And then she'd have a dozen conflicting opinions and people with too many theories and not enough facts. Such distractions were terribly hard to focus through.

But Sergeant Peters had offered her thoughts from outside her own head, which might be helpful.

She needed to sit. Miranda was halfway to sitting on a coffin—

"Ma'am!" The sergeant snapped it out.

"Oh, sorry." She forgot that death upset some people. They were in a plane wreck. Didn't they see that? At the moment the whole plane was shrouded in death, whether it was neatly packaged in a coffin or not.

But she moved to the side.

A row of fold-down web seats had been mounted along the hull. Because of the angle and twist of the fuselage, they were particularly uncomfortable, but she supposed that was the least of today's problems.

"You said there was a problem, ma'am. My problem is that I want to get these men off this flight and delivered to their families."

"Oh, go ahead and do that. At least the ten rows at the rear of the aircraft."

He huffed out a sound that was either relief or exasperation…or perhaps he'd been holding his breath for some unknown reason.

"The problem, sergeant, isn't the coffins. Correction, it's not *only* the coffins. How many plane wrecks have you seen?"

"This is my first, ma'am."

"Of the four previous hull losses of a C-5 while in some stage of flight, three of the planes were shattered by crash landing in fields or trees after significant mechanical problems. All three were during high-speed maneuvers of flight or takeoff and the damage was significant. The fourth was an emergency landing at Dover Air Force Base. It was attributable to engine failure and pilot error, but it was performed at the significantly slower flight profile of landing speed. It broke into four relatively neat pieces that remained close together. It had been flying at landing speeds when it impacted a field two thousand feet short of the runway."

"O-kay."

"This aircraft veered over a quarter mile to the side of the runway and still had sufficient momentum to cause this much destruction That is very unusual for a plane that was moving at landing speeds. Actually, I'll need to verify that it was."

"It looked normal to me."

Miranda actually looked up at Sergeant Peters' eyes but, thankfully, he wasn't watching her. He was looking at one of the few relatively undamaged sections of the hull.

She wasn't ready to interview eyewitnesses—that was the last step of her process.

But he began speaking before she could stop him. Mom had taught her it was rude to interrupt. It was hard to listen to this information arriving out of order. No time to write it all down, she tried as hard as she could to absorb the information.

"My team and I were waiting for the flight. It hit the runway clean—maybe kinda hard, but clean. Then there was sun glinting off the windshield for a moment and it veered aside. Instead of slowing, it seemed to accelerate. Or maybe everything was just happening in slow motion. It leaned so far into the curve that one wing was ripped off. It leaned the other way and lost the other wing. Then it crashed here." He shrugged. "How could something so fast happen so slowly? I can't stop thinking about it."

Miranda considered. When a C-5's massive wings lost lift they drooped, sagging from thirty feet to thirteen feet above the ground. A seven-point-four-degree sideways roll would be sufficient to drag a hundred-and-eleven-foot wing that had already lost its lift. She would have to spend some time to determine how much force would be required to tip a C-5 Galaxy that far.

She'd always liked the simple clarity of numbers and looked forward to that stage of writing an investigation report. But that layer of consideration would only become pertinent after completing the site investigation. Reluctantly she set it aside as a task for later.

8

SHE PUSHED TO HER FEET AND CONTINUED WORKING forward. It was just her and the sergeant now. His men were occupied with removing the passengers from the upper area and removing the first rows of coffins.

"Wait a second," Sergeant Peters called to her.

Miranda continued forward as the sergeant turned to look back.

"Something's not right here. There are more coffins than I have on my manifest."

Miranda liked being methodical, but she could see that the coffins ahead of her, the last row directly beneath the cockpit high above, were scorched on the ends facing the rear rather than the fronts as all of the others had been.

She was so intrigued that she almost fell out of the plane—straight down.

A massive hole had been punched through the decking and the hull in the center of the second-toforemost row. There was no coffin in this one spot of the otherwise uniform rows that stretched from bow to stern.

The coffins to either side had lost their chains and been flipped over and away to land against the sides of the hull.

Straight down was a two-story drop. The gap was created by where the rounded nose of the plane had ridden up on the face of the control tower as it destroyed it. Below her she could see the wall that was probably all that remained of the structure.

"Christ!" Again the supernatural invocation. This time from the sergeant.

Oh! A curse.

Commonly used to express anger, surprise, frustration, sadness, woe, as well as reverence. How was she supposed to differentiate which emotion was intended? A single emotion should be attached to a single word. It would make life so much easier.

"Somebody shot the plane."

"Possibly, Sergeant Peters, but unlikely. Note the direction of the damage. The perimeter of the puncture is bent downward."

Miranda considered the sergeant's unlikely scenario of someone outside shooting the plane. It *was* possible that a small inward hole had been made by an explosive shell penetrating the hold from below. Then, once inside, exploding dynamically enough to punch the outward hole thus masking all evidence of its initial inward passage.

"An anti-tank guided missile, such as a Javelin, has a two-stage warhead; the first would blow a hole in the outer layers of armor—or in this case the airplane's hull. Because of its lack of armor, the first stage would probably penetrate the cargo decking as well, prior to igniting the second stage. The second stage would be very destructive. I see no signs of the initial upward blast from the first stage, and the payload on a Javelin would have caused significantly more destruction."

"So, what exploded? A coffin?"

"Quite likely." Miranda looked again at the neat rows and the one un-coffined space. "Yes."

"I was joking."

"I'm not."

"You're something else, ma'am."

"Something else? Compared to what?"

The sergeant just shook his head.

9

"WHAT ARE YOU DOING?" MAJOR CHARLESTON WAS running up the steep slope of the cargo deck.

Again, Miranda saw no point in repeating herself.

"Well?" He planted himself directly in front of her.

Apparently *there* was some point. "My name is Miranda Chase. I'm the Investigator-in-Charge for the NTSB. I've been ordered by General Elmont to take care of his men."

Sergeant Peters was smiling at something behind Major Charleston's back.

She tried to step around the major to see what it was, but he moved to block her way. The large hole punched through the bottom of the cargo deck made it impossible to try in the other direction.

Miranda circled around one of the coffins, but the major just turned to face her, so she couldn't see whatever was behind him that was amusing the sergeant.

It did bring her closer to one of the coffins flipped onto its side away from the hole. Despite the heavy side latches, the top was loose and lying partly open against the curve of the hull.

She couldn't see any body through the gap.

It was wide enough that she should have.

Then a flicker with her flashlight and she saw a bright metallic flash. "Come look—"

"Sergeant, arrest this woman and escort her off the plane."

Sergeant Peters' look of amusement turned to one of surprise. Or at least his smile went away but his eyes widened. She was fairly sure those were indicators for surprise.

"I'm just an unarmed honor guard, sir."

"General Elmont instructed me—" Miranda began.

"General Elmont is in surgery at the hospital. I'm in charge now."

"General Elmont instructed me—" she didn't like unfinished sentences, "—to take care of his men. I promised. I have *not* been discharged from that promise."

"You aren't military."

"I *promised*. My father taught me that breaking promises is bad, and I've never found reason to doubt that instruction. I won't do that to the general merely because he is absent."

Major Charleston gaped at her.

"Now, I have an investigation to continue." She turned back to the sergeant.

"Just forget that shit. Don't move an inch." The major yanked out a radio. "I need an immediate SP detail inside the downed C-5 Galaxy."

His radio only crackled in response.

"SP?" Miranda asked Sergeant Peters softly while the major tried again.

"Security Police or Security Forces. Newer name for the MPs." Then he turned to address the major. "No signal getting out through the skin, sir."

"Goddamn it and goddamn you, Lady." He called on the radio again as he strode downslope toward the missing tail section.

"That won't keep him for long, ma'am. You'll want to work quickly. I don't recognize him, but I know the type."

"You said that there were more coffins than in your manifest."

"Yes, ma'am. More."

"Help me right this coffin, Sergeant."

"Why this one? Never mind, no time. Yes, ma'am."

They tried, but it didn't budge. It was pinned under parts of the wreckage. Again she looked inside, but all she could see through the narrow gap was that bright metallic reflection. The latches had been released, not broken. She shined a light at the last three coffins at the very front—all of which were properly latched. As was the one on the opposite side of the explosion's hole.

Something was different about this one.

The sergeant placed his fingers between his lips and unleashed a piercing whistle.

His men, who at the far end of the cargo bay had just lifted a coffin with a fresh flag on it, turned to look.

"This way. Double-time it."

They set the coffin down and trotted up the length of the cargo deck.

In moments, they had the tipped coffin freed and turned upright.

"Open it just a little," Miranda knelt down to check through the crack.

Sergeant Peters and one of his men raised the edge slowly.

A weak voice sounded from inside.

"I'm alive?"

10

IN THE COFFIN LAY A WOMAN PARTLY CLOAKED IN A FOIL
blanket. Her pants were scorched, and she looked worse
than Miranda had felt the day she'd found out that her
parents had died in a crash.

Sergeant Peters helped her out of the coffin.

When she sat heavily on one of the closed coffins
with her foil blanket still wrapped around her, Sergeant
Peters made no complaint. One of the sergeant's team
handed her a water bottle, which she guzzled down.

"There were *two* survivors," Miranda couldn't imagine
how, but there definitely were.

The woman nodded for a moment. Then croaked out,
"Who else?"

"General Elmont."

Again the weary nod.

"Why were you in a coffin?"

Her hair was crisped. Her eyebrows mostly lines of
ash. Various parts of her fatigues were scorched. Inside
the coffin was one of the emergency breather masks that

were normally stored down the length of the C-5 in case
of an emergency decompression.

"What happened?" the woman's voice was still rough.

The sergeant spoke first. "You're aboard a C-5 Galaxy
that landed at JBLM. It was either fired upon or there was
an internal explosion moments later—"

"The second one," the woman held up two fingers
from the water bottle, then drank some more.

"The plane veered badly, ripped off both wings, and
crashed into the control tower before catching fire."

"How long was I in there?"

Miranda entered the conversation, "I don't know
when you entered the coffin or the precise time of the
incident." Twenty minutes from the time she'd been
rerouted from Boeing Field until she'd arrived at the site.
Another twenty-nine minutes since then. Factoring in the
minimum time for General Elmont to contact the NTSB
and the NTSB to contact her—

"Just over an hour since the crash," Sergeant Peters
reported.

Oh, right. He'd been present and witnessed the crash.
She made a note in her personal notebook to remember
that eyewitnesses could provide a wide variety of
information. Then a note in the crash notebook to
remember to ask him if he knew the exact time of the
initial crash.

Or should she ask him now? It was really too early in
her data gathering process. But perhaps she shou—

"Felt like a year," the woman groaned. She brushed at
her hair, then stared at the ashen clump that had broken
off in her hand. "Glad I was passed out for part of it."

"There she is. Arrest her!" Major Charleston came back up the ramp leading a pair of Air Force police. They both had sidearms, rifles, and a large black-on-white "SF" patch on their left arms. Curious that they were called SPs when they were clearly labeled with an SF for Security Forces.

The woman looked at Miranda in some surprise.

"Miranda Chase is the Investigator-in-Charge from the NTSB, ma'am." Sergeant Peters indicated Miranda.

Since he'd already done the first part of her new introduction, she completed it. "I've been ordered by General Elmont to take care of his men."

"And she found you," Sergeant Peters finished.

"Arrest her now!"

At the major's repeated order, the two SF took a step up the inclined deck toward her.

"Belay that order," the woman called out.

The two police stopped and looked at her in some surprise.

"And who the fuck are you, Lady?"

The woman turned to Miranda with a look that she couldn't interpret. She held out a hand toward Miranda.

When she took it, the woman used their shared grip as a lever to pull herself to her feet, letting the foil blanket remain over the coffin.

Once she was upright, Miranda could feel her waver for a moment, then get steady on her feet. The woman finally let go of Miranda's hand to tap the eagle pins on her collar points—she didn't let go of her water bottle.

Miranda could see Withers stitched into the pocket of her blouse.

"At attention when you're addressing me, Major."

The major's eyes bulged for a moment, then he snapped to attention and saluted. "Yes ma'am."

Colonel Withers ignored the major's salute for a long moment, then finally returned it casually.

The major returned to standing at attention.

Miranda wondered about that pause and the lazy salute. Was the colonel still suffering from her ordeal or was there some hidden message? She thought Sergeant Peters might know, but she couldn't read anything from his expression as he filled the colonel in on the events.

The major didn't relax, but he did start looking around. Not at the plane or the coffins. Instead, he was looking at Sergeant Peters and the SFs—that *was* how they were labeled after all.

"Three coffins too many?" Colonel Withers cut off the sergeant when he reached that point in his narrative.

"Three more than were on my manifest."

"Did you count this one?" She pointed down at the hole in the plane.

"No ma'am."

"It's four then. Or it was. Where's the body? The one I had to dump so that I could hide in his coffin from the explosion?"

Miranda recalled something she'd seen and stepped back to the lip of the razor-sharp-edged hole in the bottom of the plane. The last of the foam had subsided and it revealed a badly burned corpse lying on the rubble below. It was closer to being a skeleton than a person. At least it had already been dead when it began its final ordeal.

She pointed down.

The colonel looked where she was pointing and sighed.

Miranda stepped partly aside as Colonel Withers shifted to full attention and sharply saluted the corpse lying two stories below. More respect than she gave Major Charleston?

Maybe.

Miranda turned to see if she could interpret the major's reaction.

His eyes were darting about frantically, then narrowed and focused on Colonel Withers' back.

"Whoops!" he practically shouted, then appeared to tumble forward toward the colonel.

He landed squarely against her back.

The colonel's arms flailed outward as she tried not to tumble into the sharp-edged hole.

Her dropping salute swung close enough that Miranda was able to hook their elbows.

Estimating angle of momentum from Colonel Withers' imminent fall, partially counteracted by the fifteen-degree slope of the deck and their probable weight differential, Miranda leaned back and to the left.

It wouldn't be enough, so she grabbed Sergeant Peters' belt with her free hand. The three of them managed to spin Colonel Withers clear.

Together she and the colonel tumbled into the still-open coffin.

Probably not where Colonel Withers wanted to be again so soon.

11

"DID YOU TAKE CARE OF MY MEN?" GENERAL ELMONT asked from where he lay in the McChord Clinic's bed. He'd refused to be moved to the off-base hospital. Miranda was half surprised that he hadn't taken his rolling IV stand with him and walked the seven-tenths of a mile back to the crash site.

"Yes, General. I did. With the help of Sergeant Peters and Colonel Withers."

"Where is the sergeant?"

"He's still working with the honor detail to escort the dead to their families."

"That's a good man," Colonel Withers said from where she sat on the next bed over while a corpsman fussed over her. Mostly what she needed was antibacterial salve and time to regrow her hair. "Stood up when and how it counted."

If not for the sergeant's quick action, the major probably would have died from his wounds where the jagged hole had sliced him so badly. When Colonel

Withers swung aside, the major had fallen through himself and landed beside the corpse on the rubble pile.

He'd been medevaced to Madigan Army Medical Center. And the colonel had sent the two SFs—who she also called SPs—to place him under arrest for reasons Miranda didn't understand.

"How did it happen?" General Elmont's voice was surprisingly soft.

Colonel Withers shooed away the corpsman and started to rise shakily to her feet.

"You can report sitting down, Colonel."

"Yes sir," she eased back down. "You saw me do the double check before landing, just making sure everything would be ready for the unloading of the Dignified Transfer."

The general nodded.

Miranda had been wondering what her own role here was, but now that they were delivering a report, she knew what to do and awaited her portion of the investigation.

"I was in my seat, we were on short final, when I realized that there were too many coffins. I knew a lot of these men. They were my men." Colonel Withers hung her head and Miranda respected the shared silence.

When she didn't continue, the general prodded her gently, "Go on."

"Sorry. I realized that I didn't recognize any of the front row of names or the center coffin in the second row."

"So, you thought to open a coffin in flight?"

"There was something wrong about it, sir. The flag wasn't set properly. And so, I went to fix it. In doing that, I uncovered a keypad. Mounted in the coffin's lid. I now know that it was a disarming pad for the explosives inside the booby-trapped coffin. Regrettably, I released the latches on the coffin to see if it was a locking mechanism."

"A bit rash, Colonel." Though the general's voice remained calm, he used the controls to raise his bed to a sitting position to face the colonel.

"I know that now, sir." She shrugged uncomfortably. "I raised the lid just enough to see that there were wires leading from the lid down into the coffin. That's the moment we landed. At the hard jostle, my weight was positioned such that I unintentionally flung the lid wide. I've seen IEDs before, General, and this was a nasty one —tank-sized rather than Humvee-sized. Had a ten-second delay timer. Took me down to seven to get moving. Grabbed a blanket and breather and dove into the next coffin over."

Now came Miranda's part.

"I'm reluctant to report items secondhand, sir." She pulled out the pocket recorder that she had kept running so that she could take verbal as well as written notes. After a moment of searching, she found Sergeant Peters' description of what happened.

My team and I were waiting for the flight. It hit the runway clean—maybe kinda hard, but clean. Then there was sun glinting off the windshield for a moment and it veered aside. Instead of slowing, it seemed to accelerate. Or maybe everything was just happening in slow motion. It leaned so far into the curve that one wing was ripped off. It leaned the other way and lost the other wing. Then it crashed here.

She stopped the recorder.

"The sun was at the wrong angle to glint off the windshield, General. The C-5 Galaxy was landing on Runway 34, almost due north. It was 1:37 p.m. when the plane landed, and the sun would be just west of south. The light, we can reasonably assume, was the explosion inside the aircraft, shining outward."

"Then it veered off course and accelerated? That part I don't understand," Colonel Withers was squinting at Miranda, so she kept her eyes on the general's IV drip to not lose focus.

"The abrupt course correction…" Miranda pictured it in her head.

Much of the C-5 Galaxy's control systems ran beneath the cargo deck. They would have been severed by the explosion.

But not all of the systems.

She looked up, not seeing the walls of the infirmary, but instead seeing the interlaced systems of the C-5 laid out before her. And then she remembered something else she'd seen.

12

"Oh." Miranda understood now.

"What?"

"The copilot's corpse was found thrown forward and toward the center."

She backtracked and mentally followed the scorch marks along the side of the cargo bay, on either side of the ladder leading, and finally up to the cockpit. On the copilot's flight console, the instruments were far more damaged by heat there than on the pilot's side.

The blast hadn't *swept* into the cockpit—it had *curled* into.

Like a spinning firestorm.

"The fire's maelstrom threw the copilot against the control quadrant. When the corpse is removed, you will find that the throttles for the Number Three and Four engines on the right side were advanced by the impact of the copilot's body." Because it was the only way that the corpse could have been as far forward as it had been—

thrown against the levers. His lap seatbelt insufficient to keep his broken body completely in place.

She continued the image in her head.

Landing.

A flash of light that had nearly killed Colonel Withers as she dove for safety in a coffin.

The copilot thrown forward.

Both engines on the right wing—one wouldn't be sufficient for the destruction that had followed—climbing to full thrust.

The massive plane veering so sharply that it rolled outward and ripped off the right-side thrusting wing.

The sudden weight loss of twenty tons of wing, eight tons of engines, and whatever remaining fuel had been in the wing tanks, would cause the plane to roll the other way.

Ripping off the left wing and the already weakened tail section.

Then it ran into the control tower and finally stopped, already on fire.

The fire hadn't happened because of the crash. The fire was the root cause.

No.

Technically, the explosion was the root cause and *that* had caused the fire.

Miranda laid it all out for the two officers sitting there in the McChord Clinic.

There were nods as they thought through the sequence themselves.

"I still don't understand why you arrested the major," Miranda concluded.

Colonel Withers twisted to look at her. "Because he tried to kill me?"

Miranda blinked. "Well, his saying 'Whoops' did happen prior to him falling into—"

"Lunging into me."

For once Miranda didn't know how to complete her sentence from there.

"He hoped I'd die going through that hole." Anger. That was definitely anger in Colonel Withers' voice.

"But why?"

"Ms. Chase, he was attempting to cover up a major crime."

"He *was?*"

"Four extra coffins. All rigged with IEDs if opened incorrectly. He was running a smuggling operation on Dignified Transfer flights."

"That doesn't seem very...dignified." She would never understand people.

General Elmont barked out a laugh, though she wasn't sure why.

"What was in those coffins?"

Colonel Withers held up her phone. "I've been getting reports from an EOD team—the bomb squad. Three coffins filled with smuggled Afghanistan heroin."

"What was in the fourth coffin, the one that blew up?"

"Why do you think the major was so upset?" The colonel's smile was not a pleasant one. "It was his payment."

13

"I'VE GOT SOMETHING FOR YOU." GENERAL ELMONT HAD called Miranda back down to JBLM a week later.

Flying her father's single-engine Mooney plane into an Air Force base more typically serving large jet transports was still unnerving. Though the flight controllers were very polite to her this time.

Most of the C-5 Galaxy's wreckage had been cleared. The new control tower was almost completed.

"You work fast."

"When we have to," the general acknowledged. He was leaning on a pair of crutches when he met her plane. "But that's not why I called you here."

Miranda didn't think that introducing herself was the right next step, so she wasn't sure what else to say.

A real Air Force Aircraft Investigation Board team had come to JBLM. Their study had fully confirmed her conclusions.

"The AIB guys still want to know how you did it," the

general began walking (crutching?) his way toward one of the hangars.

"How I did what?"

"They said that without your detailed report, they'd have missed a lot of what had happened. Especially with the burn patterns and the copilot being thrown against the controls. So how did you do it?"

"It...seemed obvious once I thought about it. Right down to how you were thrown clear." Miranda could still see the events laid out in her head like a continuous timeline.

The initial stress fractures in the tail section when the plane had veered abruptly but the broad rudder surfaces of the T-tail had resisted those shifts. Then the hard rotational stresses as the hull had twisted right, then left —again resisted by the towering empennage—finally snapping off the tail section and the general with it. If he hadn't been seated at the very rear, he'd have remained in the hull and probably died as had the rest of the crew. Even that conclusion had been confirmed by the pattern of stress fractures around the tail section.

"I'm glad it was obvious to someone. I'm proud of what you did to make sure my men were taken care of properly."

"It was also Master Sergeant Peters' diligence."

"You mean Senior Master Sergeant Peters."

"I do?"

"I recommended that he received a promotion and an Airman's Medal for a distinguishing act of heroism. I suggested officer training, but he says that he likes working the front lines of Dignified Transfer too much.

I'm afraid he's going to have a lot of work in these coming years."

Miranda didn't know much about the Iraq and Afghanistan Wars, but she'd read about how many aircraft had already been lost in the year and a half since their October, 2001 beginnings—twenty-one helicopters, seven jets, and three C-130 Hercules. She expected that meant the general was right.

"There, what do you think?"

Miranda wasn't sure what she was supposed to be looking at.

Inside the big hangar, a C-130 Hercules transport was up on jacks. It appeared to be receiving a new set of tires and brakes. A C-17 Globemaster had only three of its four jet engines mounted—she finally located the fourth one in a shop area at the rear of the hangar.

And off to the side was an antique. A shiny aluminum F-86 Sabrejet. It looked immaculate despite being fifty years old. The first of the swept-wing fighters. It had an open nose intake for the single, center-mounted engine and a glass canopy for a sole pilot. The six machine-gun ports around the nose had been covered over. No bombs or missiles hung from the hardpoints under the wings, only an outboard auxiliary fuel tank to either side which would vastly extend its operational range.

"I see by the wing shape that it's the Canadair Mk 5 variant, but it has the wing slats of an Mk 6."

The general was smiling, "An upgrade. You do know your aircraft, Ms. Chase. Removing the wing slats from the Mk 5 was a mistake that was rectified in the Mk 6. She was built in 1958. My father flew this plane in the early days of the Vietnam War. He bought it when she was decommissioned for scrapping. Gave her to me as a graduation present from the Academy."

"It's very pretty, sir."

The general seemed to want to admire the F-86 Sabrejet in silence.

Silence was one of the few types of conversation that Miranda understood.

It was a long while before he spoke again.

"It's yours."

She actually had to look at him, but he appeared to be serious.

"Nerve damage, Chase," he pointed at his leg. "Docs tell me that it will never recover enough to properly manage the rudder pedals."

"Oh."

"So, she's yours."

"But I'm not certified in type."

"Have you ever trained in a jet?"

Miranda nodded. She'd felt it was a key element to understanding crash characteristics. Jets handled and behaved in ways that were very distinct from propeller-driven planes.

"Well, we'll do some ground training and get you some check rides. She's a sweet aircraft and very well behaved."

Miranda turned from the general back to the aircraft. Built in 1958. The same year that the Boeing 707 was first introduced. The F-86 Sabrejet had been the primary fighter of the Korean War as well as the very early days of Vietnam. One customized variant had been used by

Jackie Cochran to be the first woman to break the sound barrier. It also boasted the highest number manufactured of any military plane in history—almost ten thousand had come off the assembly lines.

"Are you sure, General?"

"You'd better call me Joe if you're going to be flying my old plane."

"Okay, Joe."

"There *is* a price." He turned on his crutches to face her.

She forced herself to look up at his face, but couldn't quite meet his eyes. Eyes were even more unnerving than crowds.

"Keep looking after my men."

She nodded. She understood that he wasn't talking about just the dead.

No, his vision was bigger than that.

She could see his love for the aircraft under his command. *That's* what he thought was important. If he looked after the aircraft—all the aircraft—then his men would be just that much safer.

That's why she'd become a crash investigator. Every day since she'd lost her parents as a thirteen-year-old, she'd tried to make planes safer.

She stepped forward to rub her palm on the smooth curve of aluminum that made the nose's jet intake. Miranda used a firm pressure, just in case the jet felt the same way about touch that she did.

"It would be an honor, Joe. But my home runway is too short. I'll need to lengthen it."

The general just laughed.

IF YOU ENJOYED THAT,

BE SURE YOU DON'T MISS THE SERIES!

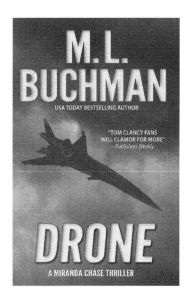

DRONE (EXCERPT)

Flight 630 at 37,000 feet
12 nautical miles north of
Santa Fe, New Mexico, USA

THE FLIGHT ATTENDANT STEPPED UP TO HER SEAT—4E—
which had never been her favorite on a 767-300. At least
the cabin setup was in the familiar 261-seat, 2-class
configuration, currently running at a seventy-three
percent load capacity with a standard crew of ten and one
ride-along FAA inspector in the cockpit jump seat.

"Excuse me, are you Miranda Chase?"

She nodded.

The attendant made a face that she couldn't interpret.

A frown? Did that indicate anger?

He turned away before she could consider the
possibilities and, without another word, returned to his
station at the front of the cabin.

Miranda once again straightened the emergency exit plan that the flight's vibrations kept shifting askew in its pocket.

This flight from yesterday's meeting at LAX to today's DC lunch meeting at the National Transportation Safety Board's headquarters departed so early that she'd decided to spend the night in the airline's executive lounge working on various aviation accident reports. She never slept on a flight and would have to catch up on her sleep tonight.

Miranda felt the shift as the plane turned into a modest five-degree bank to the left. The bright rays of dawn over the New Mexico desert shifted from the left-hand windows to the right side.

At due north, she heard the Rolls-Royce RB211 engines (quite a pleasant high tone compared to the Pratt & Whitney PW4000 that she always found unnerving) ease off ever so slightly, signaling a slow descent. The pilot was transitioning from an eastbound course that would be flown at an odd number of thousands of feet to a westbound one that must be flown at an even number.

The flight attendant then picked up the intercom phone and a loud squawk sounded through the cabin. Most people would be asleep and there were soft complaints and rustling down the length of the aircraft.

"We regret to inform you that there is an emergency on the ground. I repeat, there is nothing wrong with the plane. We are being routed back to Las Vegas, where we will disembark one passenger, refuel, and then continue our flight to DC. Our apologies for the inconvenience."

There were now shouts of complaint all up and down the aisle.

The flight attendant was staring straight at her as he slammed the intercom back into its cradle with significantly greater force than was required to seat it properly.

Oh. It was her they would be disembarking. That meant there was a crash in need of an NTSB investigator —a major one if they were flying back an hour in the wrong direction.

Thankfully, she always had her site kit with her.

For some reason, her seatmate was muttering something foul. Miranda ignored it and began to prepare herself.

Only the crash mattered.

She straightened the exit plan once more. It had shifted the other way with the changing harmonic from the RB211 engines.

———

Chengdu, Central China

AIR FORCE MAJOR WANG FAN EASED BACK ON THE joystick of the final prototype Shenyang J-31 jet— designed exclusively for the People's Liberation Army Air Force. In response, China's newest fighter jet leapt upward like a catapult's missile from the PLAAF base in the flatlands surrounding the towering city of Chengdu.

It felt as he'd just been grasped by Chen Mei-Li. Never had a woman made him feel so much like a man.

———

Keep reading at fine retailers everywhere:
Drone

ABOUT THE AUTHOR

USA Today and Amazon #1 Bestseller M. L. "Matt" Buchman started writing on a flight south from Japan to ride his bicycle across the Australian Outback. Just part of a solo around-the-world trip that ultimately launched his writing career.

From the very beginning, his powerful female heroines insisted on putting character first, *then* a great adventure. He's since written over 60 action-adventure thrillers and military romantic suspense novels. And just for the fun of it: 100 short stories, and a fast-growing pile of read-by-author audiobooks.

Booklist says: "3X Top 10 of the Year." PW says: "Tom Clancy fans open to a strong female lead will clamor for more." His fans say: "I want more now...of everything." That his characters are even more insistent than his fans is a hoot.

As a 30-year project manager with a geophysics degree who has designed and built houses, flown and jumped out of planes, and solo-sailed a 50' ketch, he is awed by what is possible. More at: www.mlbuchman.com.

Other works by M. L. Buchman: *(* - also in audio)*

Thrillers

Dead Chef
One Chef!
Two Chef!

Miranda Chase
Drone*
Thunderbolt*
Condor*
Ghostrider*

Romantic Suspense

Delta Force
Target Engaged*
Heart Strike*
Wild Justice*
Midnight Trust*

Firehawks
MAIN FLIGHT
Pure Heat
Full Blaze
Hot Point*
Flash of Fire*
Wild Fire
SMOKEJUMPERS
Wildfire at Dawn*
Wildfire at Larch Creek*
Wildfire on the Skagit*

The Night Stalkers
MAIN FLIGHT
The Night Is Mine
I Own the Dawn
Wait Until Dark
Take Over at Midnight
Light Up the Night
Bring On the Dusk
By Break of Day

AND THE NAVY
Christmas at Steel Beach
Christmas at Peleliu Cove
WHITE HOUSE HOLIDAY
Daniel's Christmas*
Frank's Independence Day*
Peter's Christmas*
Zachary's Christmas*
Roy's Independence Day*
Damien's Christmas*
5E
Target of the Heart
Target Lock on Love
Target of Mine
Target of One's Own

Shadow Force: Psi
At the Slightest Sound*
At the Quietest Word*

White House Protection Force
Off the Leash*
On Your Mark*
In the Weeds*

Contemporary Romance

Eagle Cove
Return to Eagle Cove
Recipe for Eagle Cove
Longing for Eagle Cove
Keepsake for Eagle Cove

Henderson's Ranch
Nathan's Big Sky*
Big Sky, Loyal Heart*
Big Sky Dog Whisperer*

Love Abroad
Heart of the Cotswolds: England
Path of Love: Cinque Terre, Italy

Other works by M. L. Buchman:

Contemporary Romance (cont)

Where Dreams
Where Dreams are Born
Where Dreams Reside
Where Dreams Are of Christmas
Where Dreams Unfold
Where Dreams Are Written

Science Fiction / Fantasy

Deities Anonymous
Cookbook from Hell: Reheated
Saviors 101

Single Titles
The Nara Reaction
Monk's Maze
the Me and Elsie Chronicles

Non-Fiction

Strategies for Success
Managing Your Inner Artist/Writer
Estate Planning for Authors
Character Voice

Short Story Series by M. L. Buchman:

Romantic Suspense

Delta Force
Delta Force

Firehawks
The Firehawks Lookouts
The Firehawks Hotshots
The Firebirds

The Night Stalkers
The Night Stalkers
The Night Stalkers 5E
The Night Stalkers CSAR
The Night Stalkers Wedding Stories

US Coast Guard
US Coast Guard

White House Protection Force
White House Protection Force

Contemporary Romance

Eagle Cove
Eagle Cove

Henderson's Ranch
Henderson's Ranch

Where Dreams
Where Dreams

Thrillers

Dead Chef
Dead Chef

Science Fiction / Fantasy

Deities Anonymous
Deities Anonymous

Other
The Future Night Stalkers
Single Titles

SIGN UP FOR M. L. BUCHMAN'S NEWSLETTER TODAY

and receive:
Release News
Free Short Stories
a Free Book

Get your free book today. Do it now.
free-book.mlbuchman.com

Printed in Great Britain
by Amazon

78630406R10055